To Frank Stephen Law
—W.D.M.

A heartfelt thank you to all who brought this book into being
and to all those who died in Vietnam.
—A.G.

Patrol: An American Soldier in Vietnam Text copyright © 2002 by Walter Dean Myers Illustrations copyright © 2002 by Ann Grifalconi Printed in Hong Kong. All rights reserved. www.harperchildrens.com

Library of Congress Cataloging-in-Publication Data   Myers, Walter Dean.   Patrol: an American soldier in Vietnam / Walter Dean Myers ; collages by Ann Grifalconi.   p.   cm.   Summary: A frightened American soldier faces combat in the lush forests of Vietnam.   ISBN 0-06-028363-7 — ISBN 0-06-028364-5 (lib. bdg.)   1. Vietnamese Conflict, 1961–1975—Juvenile fiction.   [1. Vietnamese Conflict, 1961–1975—Fiction.   2. Soldiers—Fiction.]   I. Grifalconi, Ann, ill.   II. Title.   PZ7.M992 Pat 2001   [Fic]—dc21   00-035009   CIP   AC

Typography by Matt Adamec   1 2 3 4 5 6 7 8 9 10   ❖   First Edition

WALTER DEAN MYERS COLLAGES BY ANN GRIFALCONI

PATROL

AN AMERICAN SOLDIER IN VIETNAM

HARPERCOLLINSPUBLISHERS

THE LAND OF MY ENEMY

has wide valleys,
mountains that stretch
along the far horizon,
rushing brown rivers,
and thick green forests.

My squad of nine men
are in the forest.

Above me, birds twitter nervously in the treetops.
Insects and small animals scurry through the underbrush,
trying to avoid the crush of my combat boots.

The squad leader raises his hand. We stop.
The sound of my breath is soft in the morning air.

Somewhere in the forest, hidden in the shadows, is the enemy.
He knows I have come to kill him.
He waits for me.

The squad leader signals, and the patrol moves out again.
The brush thickens as we head toward our target.
The fog, which rolls slowly at the edge of the forest,
is beginning to clear.
I lift my rifle and begin to rub the palm of my hand slowly
along its wooden stock.
The weather is hot, but the sweat that runs down my back feels cold.

Shots! A firefight!
I dive to the ground.
My heart beats faster.
I lift my rifle and fire into the green forest.
Bullets sing and whine over my head.
I empty my clip, sending more bullets into the trees, the bushes.

In reply, the bark flies from a tree near my head.
I think I see the enemy.
I reload and shoot again.
It is only a shadow, but I do not stop shooting.
In war, shadows are enemies, too.

Suddenly, there is silence.
We are afraid to move.
We are more afraid not to move.

I hear the sounds of the birds again.

I wonder if they speak of us from the high branches.

I wonder if what they see makes them sad.

I am so afraid.

I want the enemy to be more afraid.

I want him to tremble more than I tremble.

The radio crackles in my hand as I call for bombs.

Crouched against a tree older than my grandfather,
I imagine the enemy crouching against
a tree older than his grandfather.

We wait. We wait.
Images of those I love come to mind.

Still we wait.

Then we are startled by the sound of planes.

We look up at them and see their shadows spreading

over the valley's edge toward us.

They pass us and do their work.

The bombs explode, rumbling like thunder

at a distance that is never distant enough.

My body shakes.

I tell myself that I will not die on this bright day.

Against the horizon, columns of blue-gray smoke rise.

Two clicks away, there are flashes of gunfire.

Two clicks is the distance of my enemy.

My chest tightens.

I wipe my sweaty palms.

I bite back my tears.

We move again.
We are always moving.
My legs ache.
My shoulders sag.
My thousand eyes look for death
in the waving bamboo fields.

A village.
It is our target.
We circle it.
We swing around, sweeping our gun sights
along the windows in the huts.
We rush in behind the hollow booming of grenades.

"Secure the village!" a sergeant calls.
He points toward the enemy.

The enemy.
A brown woman with rivers of age etched deeply into her face.
An old man, his eyes heavy with memory.
And babies. Babies.
Little enemies crying on the mud roads.
Little enemies with tears running down dusty cheeks.

But I know there are other enemies.
They are strong, and young.
I am strong, and young.

The others, they are the real enemy.
They have dogs that bark at danger.
And wooden bowls that hold a day's rice.
And grandmothers who stand sullen at their huts.
This is my enemy.

The pickup zone is just beyond a rice paddy.
In the paddy, a farmer squats, waiting for the squad to pass.
His stick-thin legs disappear into the shallow water,
and it looks as if it is he who grows there.
He is the harvest we must understand.

A shot!

I reach for the ground and scramble for cover.

The elephant grass cuts my arms as I slide toward a low wall.

Then, there is an opening in the tall grass, and I look through.

There is the enemy!

He is looking at me!

We are surprised to see each other.

Shocked.

How young he is.

We stare across the distance.

I know he wants me to lift my rifle, to be the enemy.

I want him to lift his rifle.

I want him to turn away.

In a heartbeat, we have learned too much about each other.

The *putt-putt* of the chopper interrupts the moment.
The enemy turns away and is swallowed by
the lush grass that is everywhere in this land.

I lift my rifle.
I aim at the distant shadow.
I am the enemy.
I lower the rifle.

My fingers clutch the webbing of the chopper.
It strains with the weight of the squad.
Below us the land becomes a peaceful patchwork
of greens and blues and browns.

This land has wide valleys, mountains that stretch
along the far horizon, rushing brown rivers,
and thick green forests.

And war.

We land.
I am glad that I am alive.

As the heat of day passes to the heat of night . . .

. . . I write a letter to someone I love.
I wonder if my enemy is writing a letter.

I am so tired.
I am so very tired of this war.